the **BAD GUYS**

EPISODE

1

SCHOLASTIC

FOR MY BOYS

Published in the UK by Scholastic, 2022
Euston House, 24 Eversholt Street, London, NW1 1DB
Scholastic Ireland, 89E Lagan Road,
Dublin Industrial Estate, Glasnevin, Dublin, D11 HP5F

Text and illustrations © Aaron Blabey, 2015
First published by Scholastic Press, a division of Scholastic Australia in 2015
This colour edition first published in 2022.
This edition published under licence from Scholastic Australia.

ISBN 978 0702 31434 6

A CIP catalogue record for this book is available from the British Library.

Printed by Bell and Bain Limited, Glasgow
Paper made from wood grown in sustainable forests
and other controlled sources.

3 5 7 9 10 8 6 4

www.scholastic.co.uk

Design by Nicole Stofberg. Colour by Sarah Mitchell.

AARON BLABEY

WITH COLOUR BY SARAH MITCHELL

the BAD GUYS

EPISODE 1

Good deeds.

whether you like
it or not.

CHAPTER 1

MR WOLF

Pssst!
Hey, you!

Yeah, you.

Get over here.

I said,

GET OVER HERE.

What's the problem?

Oh, I see.

Yeah, I get it . . .

You're thinking,
'Ooooooh, it's a big, bad, scary wolf!
I don't want to talk to him!

He's a **MONSTER**.'

Well, let me tell you something, buddy—
just because I've got

BIG POINTY TEETH and **RAZOR SHARP CLAWS**

. . . and I *occasionally* like to dress up
like an **OLD LADY**, that doesn't mean . . .

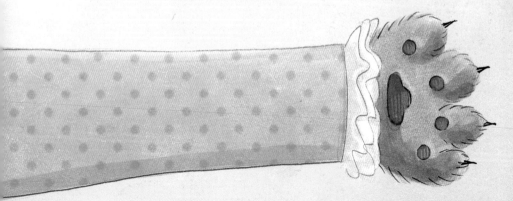

. . . I'm a

BAD
GUY.

METROPOLITAN POLICE DEPARTMENT

SUSPECT RAP SHEET

Name: Mr Wolf

Case Number: 102 451A

Alias: Big Bad, Mr Choppers, Grandma

Address: The Woods

Known Associates: None

Criminal Activity:

* Blowing down houses (the three pigs involved were too scared to press charges)

* Impersonating sheep

* Breaking into the homes of old women

* Impersonating old women

* Attempting to eat old women

* Attempting to eat relatives of old women

* Theft of nighties and slippers

Status: Dangerous. DO NOT APPROACH

It's all **LIES**, I tell you.

But you don't believe me, do you?

Because I'm The Bad Guy, right?

I'm a great guy. A *nice* guy, even.

But I'm not just talking about ME . . .

I've got some buddies who have the same problem, so I've asked them to join us.

Any minute now, they'll be walking right through that door.

They're great guys. But just like me, they are **MISUNDERSTOOD**.

So don't go anywhere, OK?

No, seriously. Don't even think about it.

CHAPTER 2

THE GANG

OK. Are you ready
to learn the truth?

You'd better be, baby.

Let's see who's here,
shall we?

Heeey! Look who it is!
It's my good pal,

MR SNAKE.

You're going to *love* him.
He's a real . . .

. . . sweetheart.

METROPOLITAN POLICE DEPARTMENT

SUSPECT RAP SHEET

Name: Mr Snake

Case Number: 354 22C

Alias: The Chicken Swallower

Address: Unknown

Known Associates: None

Criminal Activity: * Broke into Mr Ho's Pet Store

* Ate all the mice at Mr Ho's Pet Store

* Ate all the canaries at Mr Ho's Pet Store

* Ate all the guinea pigs at Mr Ho's Pet Store

* Tried to eat Mr Ho at Mr Ho's Pet Store

* Tried to eat the doctor who tried to save Mr Ho

* Tried to eat the policemen who tried to save the doctor who tried to save Mr Ho

* Ate the police dog who tried to save the policemen who tried to save the doctor who tried to save Mr Ho

Status: Very Dangerous. DO NOT APPROACH

Look at this face!
Is this the face of a monster?

I don't think so.

This is **ONE SWEET GUY**.

Will this take long, man?
I've got mice to eat.

HAHA HAHA!

What a joker this guy is!

'I've got mice to eat!'
That's a good one.

What a wise guy.

HA HA HA. HA. HA.

Hey! Who's that?
What's going on here?

Take it easy.
Have a cupcake.

A cupcake?
You got
any mice?

Enough with the mice,
or I'll

EAT
YOU!

I mean . . .

Well, well. If it isn't

MR PIRANHA.

Now, if anyone has
a bad reputation,
it's this guy . . .

Hola.

METROPOLITAN POLICE DEPARTMENT

SUSPECT RAP SHEET

Name: Mr Piranha

Case Number: 775 906T

Alias: The Bum Muncher

Address: The Amazon

Known Associates: The Piranha Brothers Gang 900,543 members, all related to Mr Piranha

Criminal Activity:

* Eating tourists

Status: EXTREMELY Dangerous. DO NOT APPROACH

Hey there, **MR SHARK**.
How's it going?

I'm

HUNGRY.

You got any seals?

Okey dokey. Nothing to see here . . .

METROPOLITAN POLICE DEPARTMENT

SUSPECT RAP SHEET

Name: Mr Shark

Case Number: 666 885E

Alias: Jaws

Address: Popular Tourist Destinations

* Will literally eat ANYTHING or ANYBODY.

RIDICULOUSLY DANGEROUS. RUN!
SWIM! DON'T EVEN READ THIS!

Status: GET OUT OF HERE!!

See?! This is what I'm talking about! How will anyone take us seriously as

GOOD GUYS

if all you want to do is

EAT EVERYONE?

What am I **TALKING** about?

Well, sit down and I'll explain.

And that means *you*, too.

the GOOD GUYS CLUB

AAAAIIIEEEE

Typical . . .

Hey, shouldn't you two be in water?

I'll be wherever I want.
Got it?
Me too, chico.
See? This is why I don't work with fish.

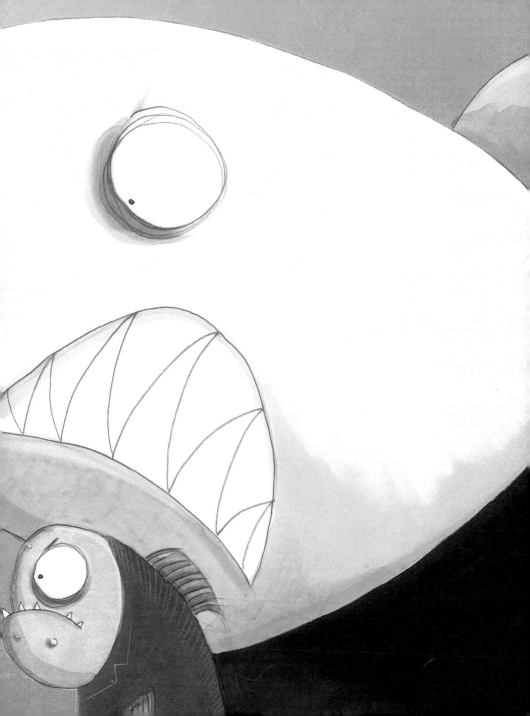

Because **THIS** is the very first meeting of . . .

THE
GOOD
GUYS
CLUB!

That's right!

The

GOOD
GUYS
CLUB!

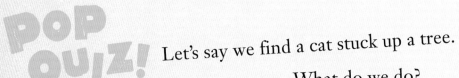

OF COURSE YOU ARE!

And I have the solution!

POP QUIZ!

Let's say we find a cat stuck up a tree.

What do we do?

This guy's loco.

No, I'm not!

I'm a GENIUS!

And I'm going to make us all

HEROES!

You'll be glad you did, Mr Piranha.

And so will you, Mr Shark.

This is going to be AWESOME.

Now, everybody climb aboard!

And let's go do some

GOOD!

· CHAPTER 4 ·
CRUISING FOR TROUBLE

This car is a fuel-injected,
200-HORSE-POWER,
rock'n'rollin' chariot of
flaming **COOLNESS**, my friend.
If we're going to be good guys,
don't you think we should
LOOK GOOD too?

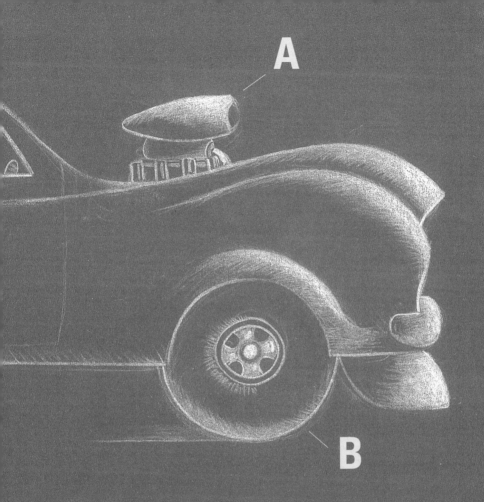

A - 'Fully Sick' V8 Engine that runs on undiluted panther wee.

B - Fat Wheels for just looking insanely cool.

C - Custom Ejector Seats for personal safety and also practical jokes.

D - Oversized Muffler for being very, very loud at all times.

We're looking for trouble, my friend. If we're going to be heroes, we **ALWAYS** need to be on the lookout for trouble . . .

We need to
be able to
SMELL
trouble!

In fact . . . wait a second . . .
I think I can smell trouble
right now . . .

Wow, it's really strong, actually . . .

Hang on. That's not . . .

AW, WHO FARTED?!

Actually, that feels quite nice.

Seriously though, man . . . what are we looking for?

CREEECH!

THAT is what we're looking for, Mr Snake!

· CHAPTER 5 ·
HERE, KITTY

So, what are we going to do?

Rescue the cat.

And what are we **NOT** going to do?

Eat the cat.

THAT'S RIGHT! I don't know about you, but I feel PUMPED!

OK, now let's do this thing . . .

What was *that*? Are you trying to give him a heart attack?

WHAT? I was, like, being totally cool . . .

Let me handle this.

HEY, YOU!
Get down here, or I'll SHIMMY up that tree and BITE you on your FURRY LITTLE BUTT!

This is not what
I had in mind.

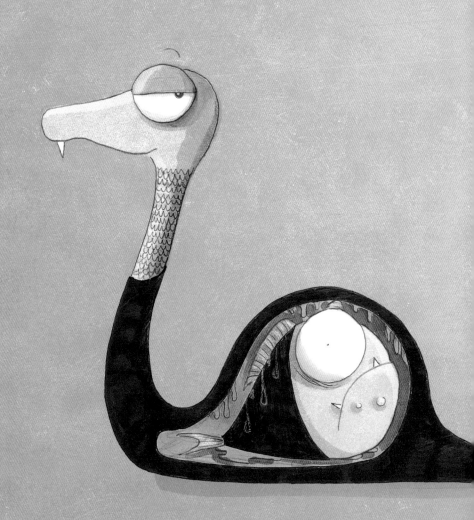

NOW,

please don't be **alarmed.**

IT'S TRUE,

snakes can be tricky and they do tend to

swallow things that take their fancy.

BUT—luckily, they swallow them *whole*

and I happen to know a gentle,

harmless technique that'll fix this right up.

Excuse me for one moment . . .

I SAID . . .

WHERE'S

THE PIRANHA?!

Hey, chico.
What's cookin'?

· CHAPTER 6 ·
THE PLAN

Nice work.
High fives,
all 'round!

You're the only
one with hands.

Fair enough.

GROUP HUG?

I don't hug. I bite. So **BACK OFF**, Mr Snuggles.

Okey dokey . . .

Ready for what?

Well, I don't know about you, but I'd say we're **READY**.

93

Our first mission.

It's time for

OPERATION DOG POUND!

THE

200 DOGS

534   10

DOG POUND

20 GUARDS

ONE WAY IN.
ONE WAY OUT.

IRON BARS!
RAZOR WIRE!
BAD FOOD!

There are 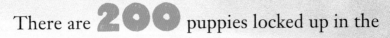 puppies locked up in the

MAXIMUM SECURITY
CITY DOG POUND.

Their hopes and dreams are trapped
behind walls of stone and bars of steel.

But guess what?

We're going to

SET THEM FREE!

We couldn't get a kitten out of a tree. How are we supposed to bust out 200 dogs?

It's easy! One of us just has to get in there and open the cages!

And how do we do that?

With **THIS!**

Are you going to dress up like an old lady AGAIN? It doesn't work, man. You ALWAYS get caught!

Who said anything about *me*?

· CHAPTER 7 ·
THE POUND

Hullo?
Oh, certainly Miss.
I'll buzz you in.

BUZZ!

Now, what can I do
for . . . uh . . . you?

I'm just a pretty young lady who has lost her dog.
Please, oh please, can you help me, sir?

He's in!
I **KNEW** this
would work.

Now, you know what to do.
Once those cages are open,
we won't have long,
so don't mess it up.

Climb aboard, fellas!

What's that
thing for?

Never you mind. Just hold on **tight.**

And **remember** — once Mr Shark gives me the signal,

I'll get you inside and all you have to do is tell the

dogs which way to run. 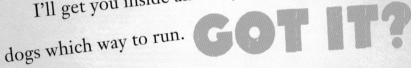 **GOT IT?**

Yeah. But
how do we
get inside?

But don't worry!

I have **EXCELLENT** aim

and I'm **85%** sure

that I'll get you in on my first throw—

THAT'S

how confident I am!

You know, I wouldn't normally open all these cages at once, but since you asked so nicely . . .

Well, here's the last cage.
Is THIS your dog?

NO!

Oh, woe is me!
I shall never find
my dog!

OH,
BOO HOO!
BOO
HOO!

BOO HOO! BOO HOO! BOO HOO!

That's the signal!

Hey, man, can we talk about this for a second?

There's no time to talk! Hold on tight, little buddies.

It's time . . .

to go

BE A HERO!

SWOOSH!

OK.
Best out of three.

YEAH.
I'm getting the
hang of it now . . .

SPLAT!

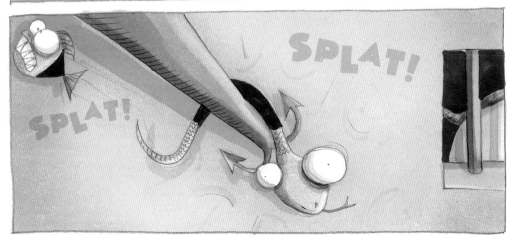

I'm sorry, young lady, but I'd better lock these cages back up now.

If we survive this, I'm going to *eat* that wolf.

Not if I do first.

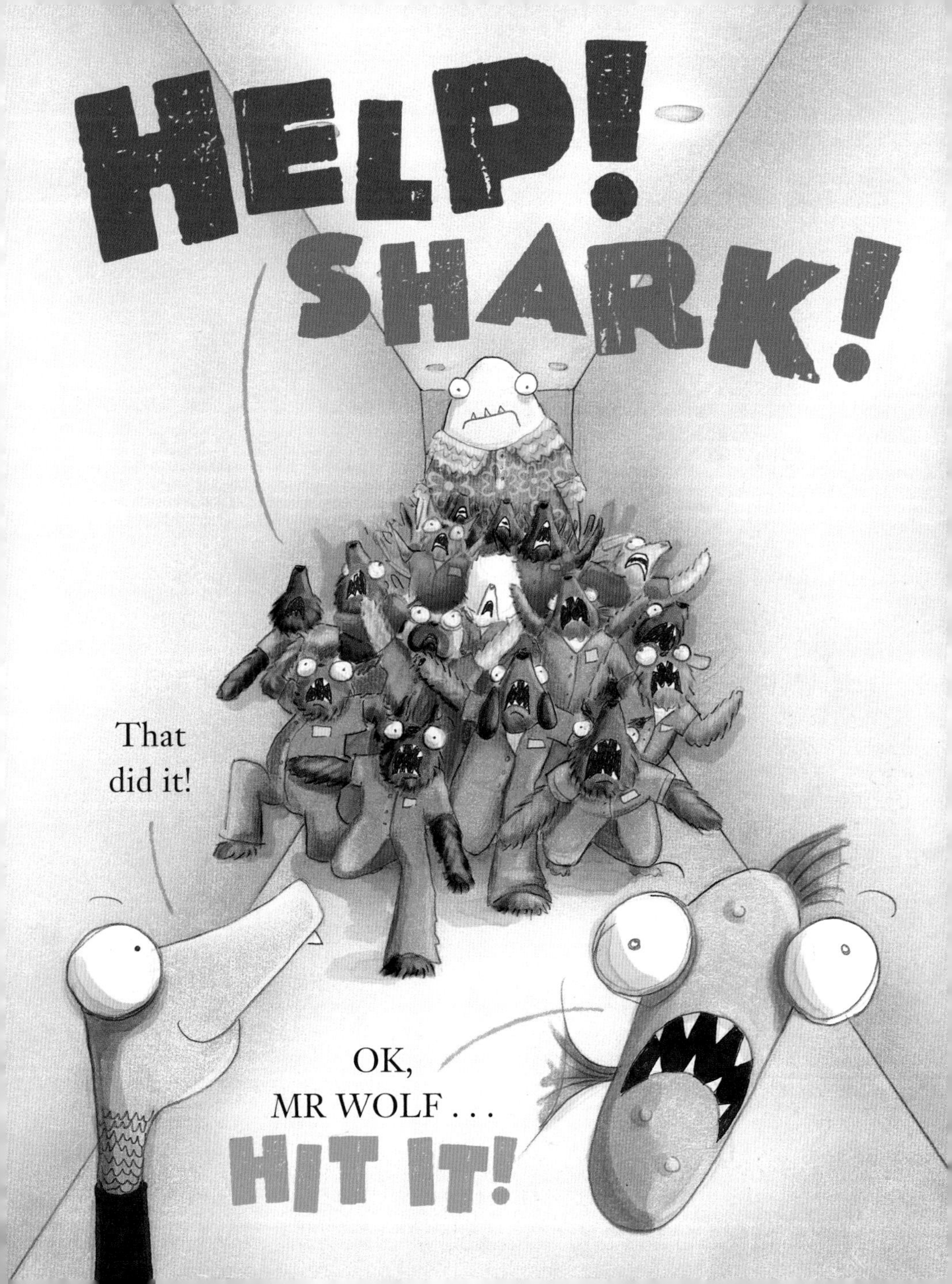

HELP! SHARK!
That did it!
OK, MR WOLF . . .
HIT IT!

I hear you,
little buddy.

Let's give those puppies their . . .

And a
SHARK! And a **SNAKE!**

And possibly
some kind of
VAMPIRE SARDINE!

224

CHAPTER 8

SO, HOW ABOUT IT?

Aw, C'MON!

You loved it! I KNOW you did!
Tell me the truth – didn't it feel **great** to be
the **GOOD GUY** for once?
Tell me how it felt, fellas . . .

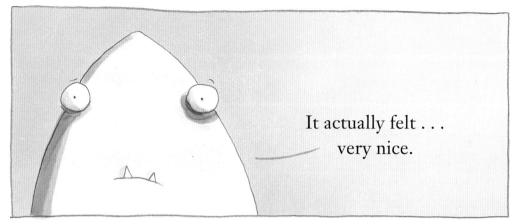

It actually felt . . .
very nice.

It felt better than nice.
It felt . . . good.

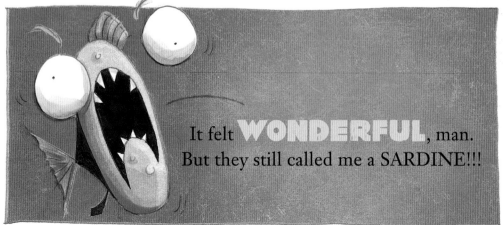

It felt **WONDERFUL**, man.
But they still called me a SARDINE!!!

If you stick with me, little buddy, no-one will mistake you for a sardine ever again! You'll be Bolivia's most famous hero! Are you with me?

Sure. But you'd better be right, chico.

And what about you, big fella?

I . . . I really liked being good. I'm in.

That just leaves you, handsome. What do you say? Want to be in my gang?

Only if I have your word that there'll be no more hugging.

I'll try, baby! But I'm not making any promises!

Today is the first day of our **new** lives.

We are **not** Bad Guys anymore.

WE'RE
GOOD GUYS!

And we are going to make the
world a **better** place.

TO BE CONTINUED . . .

GUESS WHAT?

The **BAD GUYS** haven't even warmed up.

Freeing 200 dogs is **NOTHING**.

How about rescuing **10,000 chickens** from a **High-Tech Cage Farm** protected by the world's most **unbeatable** laser security system?

BUT how do you rescue chickens when one of you is known as **'The Chicken Swallower'?**

Join the **BAD GUYS** when they return for more dodgy **good deeds** with a new, creepy member of the team . . . and keep your eyes peeled for the **SUPER VILLAIN** who just might be the end of them.

EPISODE **2**
IN FULL COLOUR

COMING SOON!